The Enchanted Snow Globe Collection

Book One – Return To Coney Island

Melissa Stoller

Pictures by

Callie Metler-Smith

THE ENCHANTED SNOW GLOBE COLLECTION
Book One – Return To Coney Island

Summary: When twins Emma and Simon shake their grandmother's snow globe during an ordinary sleepover, they are transported back to Coney Island in 1928, just in time to ride the Cyclone roller coaster and make sure their great-grandparents meet on the Coney Island trolley.

Clear Fork Publishing
P.O. Box 870
102 S. Swenson
Stamford, Texas 79553
(325)773-5550
www.clearforkpublishing.com

Printed and Bound in the United States of America.

ISBN - 978-1-946101-22-8
LCN - 2017941974

To my parents, Connie Berger and the
late Harry Zevi Berger, who taught me to read, write,
and love stories.

To my husband, Larry, whose love and support mean so
much as we travel through life's enchanted adventures
together.

To my children, Zoe, Jessie, and Maddie, who inspire
me every day. Always make good things happen!

And finally, to my grandparents, the original Jessie and
Jack Mandel. If they had not met on a trolley in Coney
Island, I would not have written this book!
- M.S.

To Logan, Ben, and Sadey...May you always find
the magic in everything. - C.M.S.

Author's Note

When I was a little girl, my favorite phrase was, "Tell me a story!" My parents told stories about their childhoods and they created long-running adventures as well. My Nana, the original Jessie, had many exciting tales to tell. I always asked to hear about the time she threw peanut shells on a handsome stranger's lap on the Coney Island trolley. That handsome man was my Grandfather, Jack.

Thank you to my Nana Jessie for sharing her stories, again and again.

Thank you to my mother, Connie (Jessie and Jack's daughter), who patiently told me endless stories and who continues to read and expertly edit every story I write.

And thank you to Callie Metler-Smith, who has helped me bring this story to life, with her beautiful illustrations and as the publisher of Clear Fork Publishing (Spork).

Table of Contents

Chapter 1

The Sleepover

"Ha, I won again," said Emma. She reached her grandmother's apartment door just before her twin brother, Simon.

"Only because you pushed me out of the way," said Simon, laughing.

The twins both rapped on the door using the secret knock: twice quickly, and twice slowly.

Their parents joined them, holding the sleepover bags. They lived in New York City, only a few blocks from Nana, but overnights were still an adventure.

Nana opened the door and reached out to hug Emma and Simon. The smell of cinnamon floated through the rooms. Simon's tummy rumbled. Nana baked the best apple crisp using an old family recipe.

"Don't forget to brush your teeth," said Mom.

"Now, don't give Nana any trouble," added Dad.

"Oh, they won't," said Nana, smiling. "I have plenty planned for the evening."

Mom and Dad handed them their bags, gave them each a kiss, and left to go to a fancy party. Loud barking echoed from the back rooms as the twins raced inside to pet Molly, Nana's puppy, who was half Maltese and half Shih tzu.

Belly rub time!

After playing with Molly for a while, the twins told Nana about a project they were working on for school.

"We need to research our ancestors and present a project to our classes," said Emma. "Can we see some of your old photos, Nana?"

"Of course," said Nana. "Let's grab the albums from my bookshelf."

"I know what would make our ancestors come to life." Emma plopped down on the couch. "A photo collage!"

"Great idea," said Nana. "And I also have cards and checkers for later. No TV or phones, you two."

"Oh, don't worry," said Emma. "I can't wait to beat you in rummy, Nana!"

"How about backgammon?" asked Simon.

"We'll get to it all," Nana said, chuckling as she reached for an album. "In the meantime, look at these photographs of your mother when she was a little girl."

"She's younger than we are!" exclaimed Emma.

She and Simon had just turned nine.

Nana pointed to a photo of a man and a woman standing on a boardwalk. The wind blew hair across the woman's face and the man reached out to brush it away.

"These are my parents, Jack and Jessie," explained Nana. "Your great-grandparents. I wish you had known them."

"What are they standing in front of, Nana?" asked Emma.

"Oh, that's the Cyclone roller coaster in Coney Island," said Nana. "It's one of the most famous roller coasters in the world. My parents met in Coney Island, you know."

"I love that story. Tell it again!" said Emma. Nana told lots of stories. This was Emma's favorite.

"Maybe we can write about this for our ancestor report," suggested Simon.

Over dinner, Nana told the story of how her parents Jessie and Jack met in Coney Island, at the tip of Brooklyn, New York.

"It was Jessie's eighteenth birthday, Sunday, June 24, 1928. She spent the day with her younger sisters, Pauline and Anna, at the giant amusement center in Coney Island. She picked that spot because Jessie loved to eat hot dogs and ride the Cyclone roller coaster, which had opened the year before.

Jessie wore her favorite blue and white short dress with a blue hat. She and her sisters took the trolley home from Coney Island to Sheepshead Bay. A handsome young man with piercing blue eyes and suspenders sat down next to Jessie. She threw peanut shells onto his lap to attract his attention and then invited him home to her birthday dinner. The handsome man's name was Jack. He and Jessie were married a few months later."

"It's so funny that she threw peanut shells on his lap." Emma cut into her meatloaf.

"And took him home," Simon added, between forkfuls of rice.

"Yes, people wouldn't do that today, but back then, it was a different world," said Nana.

"Boy, I wish we could meet them," said Simon, sighing. "I wonder what they were like." Emma agreed, turning her head to the side and imaging what her great-grandparents would have talked about on that trolley ride. She twisted her napkin on her lap as she thought about that conversation.

"You know, I have a Coney Island Cyclone snow globe in my collection," said Nana. "Let's find it in the curio cabinet."

The massive curio cabinet took up an entire wall in the living room. It reached to the ceiling and was made from a dark mahogany wood with thick shelves. Carvings of flowers, leaves, and curlicues covered the outer panels.

Nana used a large silver key to unlock the door. The cabinet was filled with snow globes Nana had collected over

the years. Big and small globes, filled with water, snow sparkles, and scenes of different places. The twins had never paid too much attention to the collection, but now they were curious.

They leaned forward to get a closer look.

There it was. The Concy Island snow globe with a replica of the Cyclone roller coaster inside. Emma blinked. She noticed a glimmer of light in the snow globe but when she peeked again, it was gone.

"Simon, did you see that?" she whispered.

"What?" he asked.

"I thought I saw light inside that globe, but I must have imagined it."

Simon stared. This time, he saw something, too. Nana carefully took the snow globe off the shelf.

Simon and Emma took turns holding the snow globe. The glass was thick and the base solid.

"This sure is heavy," said Emma, as she shook it up and down.

The Cyclone appeared almost lost amid the floating snow and swirling sparkles. Then Emma and Simon saw snow particles and swirling silver sparkles dancing in the air outside the globe. How could that be?

Emma shook her head quickly. Simon shut his eyes tightly and opened them again. The snow and sparkles lingered in front of them. The twins reached out to touch the cold, whirling specks. Emma gasped. Simon staggered and grabbed her hand. What was happening?

Up, up, up they floated. They were twirling through the air.

Flying through space.

Turning around and around, they saw Nana, small and far away.

After a few moments, a huge roller coaster appeared in front of them as they gently landed on solid ground.

Chapter 2
The Cyclone

"Where are we?" asked Emma, pacing back and forth along a boardwalk. Her heart beat fast as she gripped Simon's arm.

She didn't hear Molly barking or smell cinnamon and apples baking. They weren't in Nana's apartment anymore.

The last thing Emma remembered was shaking the Cyclone snow globe. But where was it? It wasn't in her hand any longer.

Instead, in front of them loomed the actual roller coaster. Crowds of people walked along a boardwalk. The sun shone brightly, and seagulls screeched overhead.

"Wow," said Simon. He craned his neck and stared at the roller coaster with round eyes. "Are we really in Coney Island? No way!"

They glanced at each other in surprise. They looked very different. Emma wore a short red dress and black shoes.

Simon wore short pants, a white shirt, and laced-up shoes. Emma carried a small purse she had never seen before. She poked around inside and found a pad, a pencil, and some money!

"Uh, what's going on?" Simon asked.

They hurried over to the giant coaster. A man stood outside a booth selling tickets to the Cyclone. He wore a red top hat, white pants with a blue stripe down each side, and a blue jacket.

"He looks a little old-fashioned," said Simon. "And so do we. What happened to us?"

All around them ladies in multi-colored dresses and hats passed by.

"Let's walk around a bit and figure this out. There has to be a logical explanation for why we're here," said Emma.

Emma loved finding clues that would help her solve puzzles and get answers.

She knew there was a reason they were in Coney Island.

The amusement park stood tall right next to the beach. The ocean sparkled in the afternoon sunshine. The sand shimmered with reflected sunlight. A light breeze sent gentle ripples across the flags lining the amusement park entrance.

A young woman strolled along the boardwalk in a blue and white dress and a blue hat. She looked like she was about eighteen years old. Two younger girls walked next to her.

"She looks so familiar," said Simon.

"She sure does," said Emma. "Let's follow her."

The young woman and the girls ambled away from the boardwalk and finally stopped to eat a hot dog from Nathan's. The twins watched, their faces bunched up with puzzled expressions and furrowed brows. At that moment, the young woman in the blue and white dress turned around and headed toward the Cyclone with the two younger girls trailing behind her.

"Come on," the young woman shouted. "Let's get in line for the Cyclone. I'm ready to ride!"

"Are you thinking what I'm thinking?" asked Emma. "Is that Great-Grandmother Jessie?"

Chapter 3

Jessie

"Could that really be our great-grandmother?" asked Simon. "She does look like the girl in the picture Nana showed us."

"Let's follow her to the Cyclone," suggested Emma. "I have a pad and pencil in this bag, I'll record some clues."

"I wish you had your phone in that bag. We could call Nana!"

"Uh, there were no cell phones back in the old days. But I'll take notes. Otherwise I'll never remember all these details."

Emma wrote:

Girl with blue and white dress and blue hat

With two younger girls

Eats hots dogs

Riding the Cyclone

Simon jabbed Emma lightly on the arm and said, "Hey, stop taking notes, let's buy tickets so we can keep watching them. Get on line and I'll be right back."

"Wait, I found money in my purse, take these coins."

Emma strode to the back of the line behind the girls. She heard the older girl say to the little girl, who looked to be around their age, "Anna, are you excited to ride?"

That was the name of Great-Grandmother Jessie's little sister! Another clue!

But where was Simon? What was taking him so long to buy the tickets? Emma stepped out of line but didn't see him so she scooted right back. She couldn't lose her place. Simon needed to hurry up if they wanted to ride the Cyclone right behind the girls.

After what seemed to Emma like a long time, Simon scurried back, and stuffed the last bite of a hot dog into his mouth just as he reached Emma. Emma raised her eyebrows. Simon rubbed the mustard off his face with the back of his hand and gave her a ticket.

"I was hungry," he said, smiling sheepishly.

"Yeah, I can see that," said Emma, nudging him in the arm. "You're lucky to be back in time."

They waited and watched, and soon it was their turn. The three sisters went first and started screaming the moment they were belted into their seats.

"Are you sure you want to do this, Simon?" asked Emma.

"Uh, I guess so." Simon studied the clackety wooden tracks. "I thought you wanted to."

Simon was usually ready to do anything, but this ride did look scary.

The twins looked at each other and at the Cyclone. It rose so high and appeared to touch the clouds. They gave their tickets to the ride attendant and before they knew it they were strapped into the car.

"Ready, everyone?" said the attendant. "Hold on!"

Chapter 4

More Clues

The roller coaster took off! It started slowly and then went fast, fast, fast.

Simon screamed. Emma shrieked even louder.

Up and down, over and under. It zoomed up, turned, and then dropped time after time. The twins' stomachs lurched with each movement.

At one point, Emma's face turned a pale shade of green and Simon looked like he would be sick, but in the end they were screaming with joy. The twins stepped off, shaking and a little dizzy. It took a few moments for their stomachs to settle.

"Hey, there's the younger sister, Anna," said Emma. "Let's go say hi."

"I'm not sure. Do you think we should? "What will we say to her?"

"We'll think of something. Don't worry," said Emma. "She is our great-great-aunt, after all."

They rushed over to her.

"Wow, that Cyclone was scary," said Emma.

"Oh, yes," said the girl, smoothing her brown hair.

"I'm Emma and this is ---"

"Simon, her brother," finished Simon.

"Hello, I'm Anna. I'm here with my sisters. It's my sister Jessie's birthday today."

"So nice to meet you, Anna," said Emma. "Please tell your sister happy birthday from us."

As Anna walked over to her sisters, the twins looked at each other. More clues! When nobody was looking, Emma added them to her clue list. All the clues were pointing in one direction. It had to be their Jessie!

Then they heard a voice nearby.

"Newspaper, get your paper here," called a young boy.

Simon sprinted over.

"Could I see that newspaper, please?" asked Simon.

"Of course," said the boy. "Take a look and then buy a copy."

Simon handed the boy some change that he found in his pocket. The newspaper's date was June 24, 1928. About a year after the Cyclone ride opened.

"No way! Do you realize what this means?" asked Simon.

"Wow," said Emma. "It's definitely Jessie, it's her eighteenth birthday, and it's also the day she meets Jack!"

Chapter 5

Skee-Ball

The twins sauntered over to where Anna was standing, hoping to speak with her again.

"Time to go," yelled Jessie, sounding like a big sister. "Mama and Papa will have my birthday dinner ready by the time we get home."

"Can we pick one more ride?" pleaded

Anna. "Or even an arcade game?" asked Pauline.

"Silly girls, we don't want Mama's pot roast to burn. But all right, one arcade game."

"Good-bye," shouted Anna to Emma and Simon. "It was lovely to meet you."

"Have fun!" Emma and Simon responded in unison.

Back on the Boardwalk, the girls headed straight to the skee-ball game. Emma and Simon loved skee-ball, too. They played it at the county fair each summer. Simon especially loved to toss the ball all the way up the alley to the side, aiming for the one hundred-point hole. Sometimes his ball ended up in the twenty or ten pockets instead. He tried to avoid the zero area at all cost.

"We need to spend more time with them so we can get on the trolley together and watch Jessie meet Jack," said Emma.

"I really want to see them meet," said Simon.

Emma added, "plus, we do need to work on our school ancestor report. We'll definitely have a ton to write about!"

Emma and Simon raced over to the skee-ball game. Simon got there first this time. They picked an area across from the sisters so the trio wouldn't think they were being followed.

Simon had great aim and he scrunched up his face as he concentrated. The balls zoomed. He was racking up points and

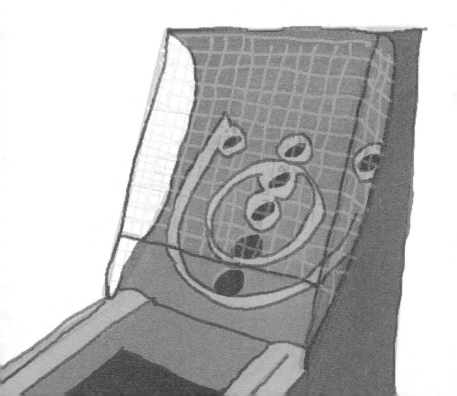

winning prize tickets. Emma took a few shots and her ball landed in the fifty slot. They were so intent on rolling the balls they almost didn't notice that Jessie, Pauline, and Anna had finished playing.

Emma leaned into her brother and whispered, "Simon, let's go!"

"Wait, I have almost enough tickets for a prize."

"The sisters are leaving," said Emma. "We can't lose them. Hurry up." She tugged on Simon's sleeve.

"Oh, all right." He frowned. "But I think that was going to be one of my best games."

The sisters ambled toward the corner of Surf and Stillwell Avenues to catch the trolley.

"We have to watch them meet," Emma said under her breath. "Come on."

They followed the three girls to the trolley stop.

Simon approached the sisters. "Hi again! We're going in the same direction. Can we ride with you?"

"Sure come on," said Anna, pointing to a nearby booth. "Buy your trolley tickets here."

"Here are some extra tickets I had from skee-ball." said Simon. He fanned out the tickets. "You can have them. I was about to win a prize, too."

"Oh, thank you!" said Anna. "I'll use them to get something lovely next time."

The twins looked for Jack on the trolley, but too many people bumped into them while getting on and off at this stop. So far, no sign of him.

"I'm so excited to watch Jack and Jessie meet," whispered Emma. "We'll have so many details to include in our report!"

And maybe they would get a clue about why Jessie decided to throw peanut shells on Jack's legs.

"This day has been perfect so far," said Simon. "What could possibly go wrong now?"

Chapter 6
The Trolley

The trolley bumped along as it moved away from the stop. It clacked quickly down the street. Most people were sitting but some were standing, hanging onto poles and straps.

A little boy in a brown cap asked if anyone wanted a shoeshine.

Another boy was selling apples. The three sisters sat leaning on each other, tired after a long day. Emma and Simon finally got a seat across from them.

Jessie caught Emma's eye. Emma felt a chill of excitement. She couldn't believe her great-grandmother had just looked straight at her.

Anna said, "Jessie and Pauline, these are my new friends, Emma and Simon."

"Pleased to meet you," said the sisters.

"Did you enjoy Coney Island?" asked Jessie.

"We sure did," said Simon, grinning. "We loved the Boardwalk and the Cyclone."

"Happy birthday!" gushed Emma. "Anna told us it was your special day."

"Thank you very much," replied Jessie. "It sure has been a special day so far."

The twins nodded their heads. Hopefully it would be even more special on the trolley.

"Where are you from?" Jessie asked.

Simon was about to blurt out an answer when Emma coughed slightly. Simon peeked at Emma. They were from the future but they couldn't exactly explain that. They were from New York City but not the city that Jessie and her sisters knew.

Emma said, instead, "we live nearby,

too." That seemed like the easiest answer and it was also the truth.

Now they were actually talking to their great-grandmother! Her elegant appearance had just a hint of playfulness. Her smile was bright and she looked at the twins as if she were studying their faces. She turned her head to one side and crinkled her kind eyes.

"You two do look a little familiar," she said. "Have we met before?"

"I don't think so," said Simon, gulping, and thinking there was a family resemblance.

In her head, Emma thought, we've only met you in photographs.

To change the subject, Emma said aloud, "We're also here to learn about our ancestors for our school project. We're just not sure how to do that."

"Well, when we're not sure about something," said Jessie, "Papa always tells us to believe in ourselves and make good things happen."

"Oh, your papa sounds nice," said Emma. "I'll always remember his wise advice."

Jessie smiled and nodded. "It helps me when I'm thinking about what to do next. I imagine Papa talking to me and I feel confident and ready to do whatever I can to make things happen."

And with that, a handsome young man
with piercing blue eyes and suspenders
boarded the trolley.

Chapter 7
Jack

"It has to be Jack," Emma whispered. Simon bounced his head up and down, staring at him.

The man glanced around the trolley. The twins saw his eyes settle on Jessie and he sort of half-smiled. Then he turned away quickly and took a seat right next to her. Emma kept watching. What would Jack do next?

He pulled out a newspaper and started to read. Every few moments he raised his eyes from his paper, took a quick sideways peek at Jessie, and then peered down again. Meanwhile, Jessie smiled at him and kept staring in his direction.

"He must be shy," said Emma quietly. "He isn't even talking to her. Doesn't he realize she's trying to get his attention?"

Jessie moved around a bit and fluttered her hands but the man still didn't say a word.

"This is the part in the story where Jessie throws peanut shells on his lap," whispered Emma.

"That's true, but where's the peanut man? Simon looked up and down the trolley.

"Jessie doesn't have any peanuts to throw!" Simon thought for a moment, before leaning toward Anna.

"Anna, where's the peanut man? asked

Simon, patting his belly. "I'd love a snack."

"Oh, we were wondering that too." Anna looked around. "We always love to eat peanuts on the way home from Coney Island."

"Well, there's a popcorn seller. Can we buy some popcorn?" asked Emma.

"Oh thank you, but no. Our uncle is a dentist and he always says popcorn is bad for your teeth," said Anna.

"I wonder where our usual peanut man is?"

"I sure am hungry," said Jessie, watching the stranger from the side of her eyes. "I wonder where our usual peanut man is?"

The stranger remained very interested in reading his newspaper.

The twins glanced at each other. If Jessie didn't have peanut shells to throw on Jack's lap, would he ever talk to her? Would they ever meet? And if they never met, would Emma and Simon ever be born?

Chapter 8
The Chase

"What can we do?" whispered Simon.

"I'm thinking, I'm thinking," said Emma.

"What would Mom or Dad do?" mused Simon. "What would Nana do?"

"You know, think about what Jessie just said. About believing in ourselves

and making good things happen."

And at that moment Emma glanced out the trolley window and saw a man selling peanuts. She grabbed Simon's arm and pointed. "Simon, there! Peanuts!"

"I'll get them," he said. Before Emma could even stop him, Simon hopped off the trolley and bought a bag of peanuts.

"Hurry, Simon," said Emma leaning out the window. "The trolley is starting to move again."

Simon was putting his change in his pocket. When Emma called out, he looked up and started running. The trolley picked up speed. Simon ran faster.

He reached out to grab the pole at the back of the trolley -- and missed it! The trolley pulled away, and Simon stopped running. He leaned over, panting.

Emma poked her head out the window and waved frantically. Simon started running again to catch the trolley but he couldn't catch up. The trolley braked at the next stop and Emma could see Simon still running with the bag of peanuts. The driver was about to start moving the trolley again.

Emma needed to do something or else Simon wouldn't get back on. And Jessie wouldn't have the peanut shells to throw onto Jack's lap. All she could hear in her

head was "make it happen." Emma turned and saw the sisters watching her.

"Poor Simon. He really must have been hungry," said Jessie, unaware of how important those peanuts really were.

Emma thought of a plan and sat up straight. She knew what she had to do.

"Whoa," she yelled out. "Make way, my friend isn't feeling well and I have to help her off the trolley.

Emma stood up and started talking to an imaginary friend.

"You'll be all right. You'll be fine!" she called out.

Then Emma cried, "make room," and stood up as if to help someone off, turning her shoulders to scoot through the crowd. People on the trolley car stood up. The driver hurried back to see what all the fuss was about.

Emma pretended that her friend had made it off the trolley just in time.

In the confusion, Simon finally caught up and got back on the trolley.

"Thanks," Emma said to the driver. "My friend will make it home and I'm sure she'll feel better by tomorrow."

The driver just shook his head and went back to his seat.

Everyone settled down and the trolley started moving again. Sweat was dripping from Simon's forehead but he also had a huge smile on his face.

"Peanuts, anyone?" he asked.

Chapter 9

Peanuts

"Oh, I would love some!" said Jessie.

Simon handed Jessie the bag of peanuts and sat next to Emma. The twins watched Jessie carefully. They knew what was supposed to happen in the story. Would Jessie throw the peanut shells on Jack's lap?

Jessie cracked several peanuts out of their shells. She ate a few and kept the shells on her lap.

Then she quietly picked up a few shells and tossed them onto Jack's lap.

At first, Jack didn't notice because he was reading his newspaper. But after a few more shells landed on his lap, he glanced up.

Emma and Simon sat up straight. They craned their necks to watch. Could this be the moment they had been waiting for? Would Jack actually talk to Jessie now?

"Excuse me, what are you doing?" Jack asked Jessie with a broad smile. "Can I have some whole peanuts, not just the shells?"

Jessie handed him a few peanuts and said, "Well, I had to get your attention somehow, didn't I? I'm Jessie, and today's my birthday."

"My name is Jack. Happy birthday and many more happy returns of the day."

"Thank you! And, in fact," Jessie continued, "my sisters and I are on the way home for my birthday dinner. Won't you join us?"

"Uh, uh, I couldn't. I don't have a clean shirt, and I'm not prepared for a birthday dinner. I don't even have a present," mumbled Jack.

"Oh, that's all right," said Jessie. "You can borrow one of Papa's shirts. You'll fit right in, don't worry."

"Well, maybe," said Jack after thinking for a moment.

"And I'll bake my famous apple crisp to go with my birthday cake."

"Why, that's my favorite," said Jack.

And with a shy smile and some more conversation, Jack agreed.

Emma and Simon nodded to each other. Jessie had made it happen, but they had helped, too. If Simon hadn't jumped off the trolley to buy peanuts, and if Emma had not distracted the trolley driver, Jessie would not have been able to attract Jack's attention.

Jessie and Jack smiled at each other and then turned to stare into Emma and Simon's eyes.

The twins had made a connection with their great-grandparents and with their great-great-aunts.

Emma felt her eyes get misty. Simon sighed.

Suddenly, Emma shifted in her seat.

"Did you see that?" she whispered to Simon.

Simon was about to say no when floating snow particles and swirling silver sparkles danced before them. Then Emma and Simon were caught in the cold, whirling specks. Up, up, up they floated.

They were twirling through the air.

Flying through space and time.

Turning around and around they saw Jessie, Jack, Anna, Pauline, the Coney Island trolley, and the Cyclone far away. Molly's barking grew louder. The scent of cinnamon drifting through the air grew stronger.

And they could see Nana growing closer and closer.

Chapter 10

Return To New York

In the blink of a moment, the twins stood on solid ground in Nana's living room in front of the giant curio cabinet.

Emma held the Cyclone snow globe.

Nana stood next to them, and Molly nuzzled Simon's hand. Belly rub time!

Everything was back to the way it had been.

Except Emma was still carrying the small purse with the pad and pencil inside.

"You know, my parents bought this snow globe for me when I was a girl," said Nana. "I sure loved to ride the Cyclone."

The twins stared at each other and at Nana. She seemed to have no idea about the voyage they had just taken!

"Who's ready for apple crisp?" asked Nana. "It's your great-grandmother Jessie's favorite recipe!"

When Nana walked away, Emma pulled out her pad and saw her notes about Jessie and Jack. It was real! It all did happen.

The twins smiled and shook their heads as they raced into the kitchen.

"Ha, I won this time," said Simon, laughing.

They were hungry and the dessert tasted delicious, as they knew it would!

"Ready for rummy, checkers, and backgammon, you two?" asked Nana, placing the games on the dining room table. "And the ancestor photo collages."

"We sure are," said Simon. Emma nodded in agreement.

They both yawned. It had been a long day.

The twins' parents arrived the next day after lunch.

"How was the sleepover?" asked Dad.

"What did you do?" said Mom.

"Well," began Emma slowly, "we did some research for our ancestor report about Great-Grandmother Jessie. We really feel like we connected with her.

Now we need to visit the library to find books about Coney Island."

"Why don't we go to Coney Island right now?" asked Mom. You won't believe how huge the Cyclone is and how fast it goes!"

"Uh, I think we'll believe it all right," Emma said under her breath. Simon blinked and nodded.

"And I really want to play the skee-ball game, and eat some hot dogs!" said Simon.

"How do you know that Coney Island has skee-ball games?" asked Mom.

"Uh, well, I just bet it would, that's all," said Simon, blushing. "And you know, I'm really good at skee-ball. Maybe I'll even win a prize."

As their parents were talking to Nana, Emma and Simon ventured back into the living room to take one last look at the giant curio cabinet.

"Does Nana know anything about our adventure?" asked Simon.

Emma paused. "I don't think so," she said. "Everything is the same as when we left."

Just then, Simon noticed a snow globe way in the back. A train was suspended in the snow globe, and all around the train, snow particles were shaking and shimmering. He pointed at it and Emma squinted and stood even closer to the cabinet.

"Are you thinking what I'm thinking?" asked Emma.

"Absolutely," said Simon. "Could it be enchanted too, like the Coney Island snow globe?"

Before Emma could answer, Mom shouted, "Let's go, you two."

They took one last look but all they saw were regular snow globes sitting in a giant curio cabinet.

As they hugged Nana goodbye, and petted Molly, they wondered if an adventure on a train might be waiting for them.

"Can we do another sleepover next weekend?" begged Simon.

"Oh yes, please," said Emma.

"Of course," said Nana laughing, "and in the meantime, go out and make good things happen."

The Real Jessie And Jack

The Enchanted Snow Globe Collection

Book One:
Return To Coney Island
Family Book Club Guide

Here's a family book club guide with questions for discussion, a recipe for apple crisp, easy directions to make your own snow globe (maybe featuring a place you want to visit), family connection projects, and research links to enrich the story experience.

Enjoy and happy reading!

Discussion Questions

1) If you could, would you travel in time, and if so, to what time period and place? Why? Talk about some of the ancestors that you and your family might want to meet.

2) Do you think Emma and Simon should tell Nana or their parents about their time travel adventure? What would you do?

3) Jessie tells the twins to "make good things happen" and Nana repeats the same message. Do you agree with that advice? How can you do that in your own life?

4) Look around your home, school, or library. Do you think there are any devices like a snow globe that could allow time travel? Do you think someone will ever invent a time travel machine? Should people try to travel through time?

5) The ending of the story features a clue about Emma and Simon's next adventure. Where do you think they will go and what will they find there? Where else would you like to see the twins visit? Connect with me at **www.MelissaStoller.com** and let me know what you think!

Recipe
Easy Apple Crisp

Emma and Simon enjoy Nana's Apple Crisp. Now you can make your own (with help from an adult!):

Ingredients:

4 apples (we usually mix McIntosh and Granny Smith apples)

1 stick unsalted butter

1 cup brown sugar

1 cup flour (regular or gluten-free)

Cinnamon

Directions:

1) Peel, core, and cut the applies into small slices

2) Layer the apple slices on the bottom of an 8 or 9-inch baking dish

3) Melt the butter stick

4) In a bowl, mix the sugar and flour with the melted butter

5) Pour the mixture over the apple slices

6) Add cinnamon on top to taste

7) Bake at 350 degrees for 50 minutes until the apples are soft and the topping is crisp

8) Enjoy!

Craft Project
A Homemade Snow Globe

There are many snow globe craft project descriptions online. Here's an easy project guide:

Supplies:

Glass or clear plastic jar with lid (baby food and mason jars work well)

Glue (a hot glue gun used with supervision, or a strong craft glue)

Glitter

Small plastic figurines

Glycerin (optional)

Water

Directions:

1) Glue one or two small figurines to the inside of the jar lid and let dry

2) Add water and glycerin (optional) to the jar

3) Add glitter

4) Before screwing the lid to the jar, add a little glue to avoid leakage

5) Shake and enjoy your homemade snow globe!

Family Connection Projects

1) Interview family members about your ancestors – make videos of older relatives speaking about their own family histories

2) Write a story based on your ancestors – either a biography or a fictional account

3) Take a field trip to the place your parents or grandparents met or to another place that's important in the story of your family

4)   Look through old photos of your parents or grandparents like Emma and Simon did and tell each other stories about the people in the photos

5)   Create a family heritage photo album, scrapbook, collage, or family tree

Research Links About Snow Globes, Coney Island, Roller Coasters, And Trolleys

Do you want to know more about some of the history behind the story? If so, read on:

The invention of snow globes has an

international history, with contributions from France starting in 1878, Austria in 1900, and the United States in the 1920s, 30s, and 40s.

Check out:

www.mentalfloss.com/article/71983/brief-history-snow-globes

www.nytimes.com/.../the-view-from-harrison-collector-of-6000-snow-domes-knows-

For information about Coney Island and the Coney Island Cyclone, visit:

http://www.allianceforconeyisland.org

www.lunaparknyc.com

www.coneyislandhistory.org

https://www.nycgovparks.org/parks/
the-cyclone/history

Interested in learning about the science behind roller coasters? Check out:

www.howstuffworks.com/engineering/
structural/roller-coaster.htm

Want to see pictures of the old Coney Island trolleys? Check out:

www.forgotten-ny.com/2012/03/
coney-island-trolley-poles/

http://www.thejoekorner.com/lines/
brooklyn-trolleys/bklyntrolleys-frame.
htm

Coming Soon

Where Will The Enchanted
Snow Globe Collection Take The
Twins Next?

The Enchanted Snow Globe Collection: Book Two – The Liberty Bell Train Ride

Emma and Simon shake another enchanted snow globe on their latest sleepover with Nana. This time, they're transported to Philadelphia in 1915 and witness the Liberty Bell making its last historic transcontinental train ride to San Francisco.

They soon realize that their Great-Great-Aunt Lucy was one of the schoolchildren who signed the petition bringing the Liberty Bell to California. When trouble brews, will the twins and Aunt Lucy be able to help the Liberty Bell get back on track?

ABOUT THE AUTHOR

Melissa Stoller is an avid collector of snow globes, sea shells, stories, and other treasures. She lives in New York City with her husband, three daughters, and a mischievous puppy. Her debut picture book, *Olive's Magic Paintbrush*, will be published in March 2018 by Clear Fork Publishing/Spork. In previous chapters of her life, Melissa worked as a lawyer, legal research and writing instructor, and early childhood educator. Melissa is also the co-author of *The Parent–Child Book Club: Connecting With Your Kids Through Reading* (HorizonLine Publishing, 2009).

www.MelissaStoller.com

ABOUT THE ILLUSTRATOR

Callie Metler-Smith is the owner of Clear Fork Media Group in Stamford, Texas. She has owned the Stamford American since 2009 and Clear Fork Publishing since 2014. When not working on her corner of the Stamford Square, she is spending time with her husband, Philip; two sons, Logan and Ben; and niece, Sadey.

www.calliemetlersmith.com

CPSIA information can be obtained
at www.ICGtesting.com
Printed in the USA
BVOW09s1926100817
491573BV00001B/93/P